Ants in Your Pants, Worms in Your Plants! (Gilbert Goes Green)

Diane deGroat

HARPER
An Imprint of HarperCollinsPublishers

Ants in Your Pants, Worms in Your Plants! (Gilbert Goes Green)
Copyright © 2011 by Diane deGroat
Library of Congress Cataloging-in-Publication Data is available.
ISBN 978-0-06-176511-7 (trade bdg.) —
ISBN 978-0-06-176512-4 (lib. bdg.)

Typography by Jeanne L. Hogle
17 SCP 10 9 8 7 6
❖
First Edition

Other Books About Gilbert

It was a beautiful spring day. Gilbert didn't want to be indoors. Mrs. Byrd had asked her class to write a poem about springtime, but Gilbert just wiggled and jiggled and squirmed in his seat.

Mrs. Byrd asked, "Do you have ants in your pants, Gilbert?"

"Sorry," Gilbert said. "I can't think of anything to write about." He chewed on his pencil, he looked at the ceiling, and he tapped on his head while everyone else was writing.

Patty never had trouble getting ideas. She read her poem aloud to the class:

> Spring is fun.
> Let's run in the sun!
> Let's smell the flowers
> And play in the showers.
> Spring is fun.

Mrs. Byrd sighed and said, "You're so right, Patty. It's just too nice to be indoors. Let's all bring our lunch tomorrow, and we'll have a picnic."

Everyone said, "Yay!" Even Mrs. Byrd had good ideas!

The next day Mrs. Byrd walked with her class up the big grassy hill in back of the school. She said, "When I was your age, I loved to go on picnics with my family." As she hurried up the hill, she said, "I hope we can find a place that's shady and green."

But when they got to the top of the hill, it wasn't shady or green. The trees had been cut down and the sun was hot. The grass was brown. And litter was all over the place.

"Oh dear," Mrs. Byrd said. "This is a terrible place for a picnic!"

"Maybe we could clean it up," Kenny said.

"Good idea!" everyone said as they rushed to pick up the trash.

Philip picked up cans and bottles. Lewis picked up an old shoe.

Gilbert picked up a half-eaten apple covered with ants.

When they finally sat down to eat, Mrs. Byrd said, "Earth Day is next week, and today we've already done something to make our Earth cleaner. What else can we do to help our planet?"

Gilbert didn't have any ideas about Earth Day. He was busy making sure that ants didn't crawl in his pants!

But Philip had a good idea. He said, "We can recycle those bottles instead of throwing them into the trash. They can be made into new bottles."

Patty said, "At home we can turn out the lights when no one's in the room. That saves electricity."

"And we shouldn't waste water either," Margaret added.

"Good idea," Lewis said.

"I'm not taking a bath tonight!"

Everyone said, "Eewww."

Back in the classroom Mrs. Byrd asked everyone to start working on an Earth Day project.

Gilbert groaned. Now he would have to come up with an idea for an Earth Day project! He didn't even have an idea for his spring poem yet!

Patty had already started. She drew a big lightbulb and wrote under it: *Turn out the light. Because it's right!*

"That's a good idea," Gilbert said. "I'm going to draw a lightbulb too."

"That's *my* idea," Patty said. "You have to think of your own."

Frank found a book in the library about saving energy. "Here's a good idea," he said. "We can ride our bikes or walk to school instead of driving. That saves gas. Someday the Earth might run out of fuel, so we shouldn't waste it."

Gilbert looked through the book when Frank was done, but all the good ideas had already been taken. "I don't think I'll ever get an idea," Gilbert said.

Lewis grabbed Gilbert's ear and looked inside. "I see the problem,"
Lewis said. "There's nothing in there!"

Gilbert was beginning to think that Lewis was right!

After school Gilbert said to Mother, "I need to do an Earth Day project, but I don't have any ideas."

"What about recycling?" Mother asked.

"Philip is doing that," Gilbert said.

"What about saving electricity?"

"Taken," Gilbert said. "I want to do a project that nobody else is doing, but I can't think of any."

Father said, "When I'm looking for an idea, it might come to me
when I'm walking or riding my bike. Or sometimes when I'm relaxed
or drifting off to sleep, an idea will suddenly pop into my head."

Gilbert tried walking to get an idea. He tried riding his bike. But no
ideas came.

Gilbert was about to take a nap when Mother said, "You know, a good idea can be right in front of you and you don't even know it. Try to keep your eyes and ears open, and something will turn up."

Gilbert sat very quietly under his favorite tree and kept his eyes and ears open. He listened and watched as the wind gently blew the grass. Then something caught his eye. Ants! He watched as a line of big black ants crawled from the tree to the grass to . . .

And then an idea was right in front of him.

On Monday, everyone took turns talking about their projects. Frank went first and said, "My mom and I rode our bikes to school today instead of driving. Mom says that besides saving gas, she's getting good exercise."

For Kenny's project, he had helped his dad hang the laundry on a clothesline in the yard instead of using the dryer. "That saves a lot of electricity," he said.

When it was Philip's turn, he showed everyone all the things that could be recycled. He explained, "Old paper can be made into new paper. Metal can be made into new cans. And glass and plastic can be made into new bottles." Then he said sternly, "From now on, I'm going to check the wastebasket every day to make sure nobody throws any of this stuff into the trash."

"Oops," Lewis said, taking his water bottle out of the wastebasket.

For Margaret's project, she held up a cloth bag with handles on the top and a big sun on the front. "My mom and I are making these bags to take to the supermarket instead of using paper or plastic bags that get thrown out. We can reuse these over and over."

When it was Lewis's turn, he said, "I did an Earth Day project with real earth." He opened up a box and everyone said, "Pee-yoo!"

"It's compost," he said. "It's supposed to smell bad—at least in the beginning. You can take garbage like eggshells and apple peels and mix it all with dirt, and after a while it turns into really good soil to grow stuff in." He reached in and pulled out a worm.

When everyone was done saying "Eewww," Lewis continued, "Worms help to turn the dirt into compost by eating it and pooping it out."

Everyone said "Eewww" again.

When it was finally Gilbert's turn, he held up his drawing of a tree and said, "Trees are important to our planet. They give us wood to make things like paper and furniture. And they help to keep the air clean. When too many trees are cut down, the air can get polluted and stink."

"Like my compost!" Lewis said. Everyone laughed.

Patty liked the poster and asked, "How did you get your idea, Gilbert?"

"It was right there in front of me," Gilbert said. "We see trees all the time, but we never think about what they do." Then he said, "But this is just the first part of my project. For the second part, we have to go outside."

"Field trip!" Lewis shouted.

"Where are we going?" everyone asked.

"It's a surprise," Gilbert said. They followed Gilbert up the big hill behind the school. There they found a little tree planted right where they had had their picnic.

"I found this growing under my favorite tree," Gilbert said. "I thought it was a weed, but it was really a baby tree. The principal said my dad and I could plant it here. It's small now, but someday it will be big enough to shade this hill and make it a perfect place for a picnic."

Everyone liked the little tree, especially Mrs. Byrd. She gave Gilbert a hug and said, "What an excellent idea, Gilbert!"

Then she noticed the sign hanging on the tree. Gilbert had finally written a poem:

This little tree
Will grow and blossom.
And someday you'll see
This tree will be awesome!